DaVID BEDFORD

SOCCER CAMP

Illustrated by Keith Brumpton

Removed

Kane Miller
A DIVISION OF EDC PUBLISHING

Follow the Team!

Book 1 – **The Soccer Machine**

Book 2 – **Top of the League**

Book 3 – **Soccer Camp**

Book 4 – **Superteam**

First American Edition 2006
by Kane/Miller Book Publishers, Inc.
La Jolla, California

First published in 2004 by Little Hare Books, Australia
Text copyright ©David Bedford 2004
Illustrations copyright © Keith Brumpton 2004

For information contact:
Kane Miller, A Division of EDC Publishing
P.O. Box 470663
Tulsa, OK 74147-0663
www.kanemiller.com
www.edcpub.com

Library of Congress Control Number: 2006920743
Printed and bound in the United States of America
2 3 4 5 6 7 8 9 10

ISBN: 978-1-933605-07-4

For my son, Tom
DB

Chapter 1

"We're here!" shouted Harvey.

The Team cheered as their bus turned off the main road. It swung past a white building with a sign saying "Soccer Camp" above its wide, glass doors, and stopped in a parking lot surrounded by trees.

Rita joined Harvey at the window as he watched people in yellow baseball caps setting up a small stage on a soccer field. "There are three fields!" he told her excitedly.

"Watch out!" they both cried as they were crushed against the window by Professor Gertie and Mark 1.

"Make room!" said Professor Gertie. "We want to see, too!" Professor Gertie was Harvey's inventor neighbor and The Team's biggest fan. She squeezed between Rita and Harvey.

"I can't believe we're actually at Soccer Camp," Harvey said. "This is where the real players come to practice."

"You're here because you won the league," Professor Gertie proudly reminded him.

Mark 1 stood on the seat to peer over them. He was The Team's coach, and Professor Gertie's best-ever invention: a Soccer Machine.

Mark 1 spoke in his strange mechanical voice. "Thanks, Harvv."

Harvey looked at him and jumped. "What are you wearing?!"

Professor Gertie lowered her voice as Steffi and Matt jostled past, fighting to be the first off the bus. "It's a disguise," she explained.

Rita laughed. "He just looks like a robot with a false nose, moustache and glasses!"

"No one will notice," said Professor Gertie, trying to sound confident.

"But why is he wearing it?" asked Harvey.

"Well …" Professor Gertie looked flustered, "you're always telling me robots aren't allowed to play on The Team."

"The referees don't like them," Harvey agreed.

"But Mark 1 deserves to be here, doesn't he?" Professor Gertie went on.

"Of course he does," said Rita. "We'd never won a single game until Mark 1 began coaching us."

"Well then," said Professor Gertie, as if that explained everything.

"I still don't understand," said Rita.

Professor Gertie said awkwardly, "The teams that come to Soccer Camp have to bring two 'Responsible Adults' with them. Since Mark 1 can't be on The Team, he has to be a grownup, like me."

Harvey looked at Rita, and knew what she was thinking. Even with a moustache, Mark 1 didn't look anything like a "Responsible Adult." His head was made from an upside down trashcan and, still visible behind the false glasses, his eyes were red lights, like the scanners at a supermarket checkout.

Professor Gertie looked around. "Where has everybody gone?" she asked. "They

should have waited for the 'Responsible Adults' to lead them off the bus!"

Harvey and Rita followed Professor Gertie and Mark 1 as they trotted across the parking lot, trying to catch up with the rest of The Team.

Professor Gertie kept looking around uneasily, and as they passed along the side of the white building where tables and chairs were being set up, she tried to shield Mark 1 with her lab coat.

"This is silly!" laughed Rita. "Who cares if we brought a robot anyway?"

Professor Gertie didn't say anything.

"Would we be in trouble?" asked Harvey.

Professor Gertie pretended not to hear.

"You have to tell us!" said Rita.

Professor Gertie glanced over each shoulder, then reached into her pocket and took out an envelope. "I don't think they'd actually do it," she said.

"Do WHAT?" shouted Harvey and Rita together.

"Here, you read it." Professor Gertie handed Harvey a letter. He read out loud,

"Dear Team,

Congratulations! You have won a place at Soccer Camp, the training center for professional players.

Every year, three of the best junior teams from around the country are invited to compete for the Soccer Camp Cup.

All teams MUST be accompanied by TWO 'Responsible Adults.'

Any team that breaks the rules will be sent home immediately."

Harvey's stomach felt full of nervous knots. Winning this trip to Soccer Camp was the best thing that had ever happened to him – losing the chance to play even a single game would be the worst.

"They wouldn't send us home," said Rita. "They couldn't!"

"They could," said Harvey gloomily. "And as soon as they realize Mark 1 isn't a 'Responsible Adult,' they will."

Chapter 2

"Nonsense!" said Professor Gertie. "We won't be sent anywhere as long as we don't draw attention to ourselves. Now hurry up; we're late."

Harvey shoved the letter into his pocket as he and Rita jogged to catch up with the rest of The Team. They were sitting on the field in front of a man wearing a yellow baseball cap with "Coach" written on the front. The coach had flabby cheeks and tight lips that looked like they spent most of their time blowing a whistle.

Two other teams were grouped on the ground as well, but Harvey didn't have time to check them out because the coach was wagging a finger at him and Rita.

"You're late!" he barked. "And where are your adults?"

Professor Gertie blustered up, holding Mark 1 behind her with one arm. He was jumping up and down in his built-in Bouncing Boots, craning to see over her head.

"It's lucky we haven't unpacked our bags yet," Harvey whispered to Rita, "because we're going straight back on the bus!"

The coach frowned. "Are you The Team's adults?" he asked Professor Gertie and Mark 1.

"Yep, Sssir!" declared Mark 1 at the top of an extra-high bounce.

The coach rubbed his eyes.

"Are you sure you're old enough?"

"Yep, Sssir!" said Mark 1, his false nose, moustache and glasses wobbling dangerously.

"We're definitely adults!" broke in Professor Gertie quickly. "We're very responsible, too. We're not in disguise, or anything!"

Harvey covered his face with his hands, feeling his heart thump in his chest. This was it. They were about to be sent home. But to his surprise, the coach clapped his hands once and said, "Okay teams, welcome to Soccer Camp!"

Everybody around Harvey and Rita cheered.

Harvey listened closely while the coach explained what they would be doing during their two days at Soccer Camp. The teams would play each other for the Camp Cup. And there would be a strategy session. Harvey couldn't wait for that. All the best teams had strategies. They were essential.

"The first game after lunch will be The Team against the Termites," announced the coach before leading them back to the main building, where cardboard sandwich boxes were being laid out on tables by the same yellow-capped people Harvey had seen setting up the stage.

The first team to line up was small and wiry, and each player wore a T-shirt with "The Mighty Termites" written on the back.

"They look more like 'The Tiny Termites' to me!" Steffi scoffed, and The Team laughed. Harvey had already noticed something about the Termites though.

They had formed a neat line, and as each player grabbed a box, they turned and walked back to the field in the same neat line.

"They're well-organized," he told Rita, who nodded.

Professor Gertie pushed in front of Harvey, chose a box, and bustled away, leaving Mark 1 behind. "I'm just going to get the bags off the bus!" she called.

The Team carried their lunch past the Termites and onto the empty field. Harvey made sure Mark 1 was hidden in the middle of the group when they sat down to eat.

"Look!" Darren pointed as the third team trekked past them to the other field.

"They're huge!"

"They look like a herd of rhinos," said Rita.

"Rhinos don't travel in herds," said Steffi. "Anyway, they're called the Buffalos."

"Same thing," said Rita. "We're still going to get trampled."

"No way," said Matt confidently. "They might look beefy, but The Team wouldn't be here if we weren't a match for them."

"We should make the most of it," Harvey said, watching Mark 1, who had pushed his false nose, moustache and glasses up onto his forehead to keep the sun out of his eyes. "We might not be here for very long." He took the Soccer Camp letter from his pocket and handed it around.

"Is Mark 1 supposed to be our 'Responsible Adult'?" asked Steffi after she'd read the letter, shaking her head in disbelief.

Harvey nodded.

"But when they find out, we'll be sent home!" Steffi said.

Rita tried to cheer everyone up. "We'll be okay. The coach was completely fooled by Mark 1's disguise. What could go wro--?"

Before she'd finished speaking, a blast of cold water hit her square in the face, almost knocking her backwards.

The Team all jumped up, ducking and dodging as more spray hit them.

"Where's it coming from?" yelled Harvey.

"Everywhere!" shouted Darren.

"This way!" said Harvey, making a dash for the sideline but skidding on the slippery grass. The rest of The Team tripped over him, making one big, soggy heap.

The water stopped as suddenly as it started.

Harvey felt Mark 1's metal head crushing his ribs. Wriggling out of the pile, he heard a noise and looked up.

The Buffalos and the Termites were bellowing and squealing as if they'd just seen the funniest thing in the world.

"We were supposed to be keeping a low profile!" Harvey said despairingly.

"At least it can't get any worse," muttered Rita.

Click!

"It just has," said Harvey. Someone had taken their picture.

Chapter 3

Professor Gertie came rushing up. "You're soaked! What happened?" she shrieked.

"The sprinklers must be broken again," said the coach, who was right behind her. "But don't worry, everyone has to change into their uniform for the photo shoot anyway."

"Photo shoot?" asked Steffi, her eyes widening.

"You've got five minutes," said the coach, checking his watch.

Professor Gertie led the way to two wooden huts tucked among the trees. "Boys to the right, girls to the left," she said. "I've already put your bags inside."

She took the girls away, and Harvey led Mark 1 and the boys into their hut, where they found two rows of bunk beds. Sitting neatly on each of those closest to the door was a small bag with a picture of a termite on the front.

"The Mites must have gotten here first," Matt complained.

Further in, there was a jumble of enormous backpacks.

"The Beefs," commented Matt as he stepped over them.

The Team's bags were leaning against the bunks at the back of the room.

Professor Gertie came in, holding a large bundle in her arms. "My new invention!" she declared.

Harvey handed out the shiny red shirts, white shorts, and red socks.

"Nice bit of cloth!" said Darren, who was holding up his brand new silver-edged

goalkeeper's jersey.

"My Supercloth is indestructible!" said Professor Gertie. "It never loses its shine, never tears, and never wears out."

Harvey helped Mark 1 change out of his wet clothes before slipping his own new shirt over his head. It smelled like a fresh bar of soap.

"Supercloth is coated with Self-Cleaning Sudsoap," Professor Gertie continued. "Mud and stains fall off while you wear it. I'll never have to wash filthy uniforms again!"

She hurried back to the girls' hut just as the Termites and the Buffalos barged in, changed at top speed, and stomped out again.

The Team were still struggling with their shorts. Then Professor Gertie called from the door in a high, embarrassed voice. "Er ... it seems there may be a problem with the Easy-Fix Shorts. I'll tie them up for you on your way out."

Harvey was searching under the beds. "I

can't find my bag," he told Darren as the rest
of The Team trooped out behind Mark 1.

"Hurry, boys!" called Professor Gertie.

"Just put your uniform on," said Darren.
"We can find your bag later."

"I can't," said Harvey.

"Why not?" asked Darren.

"I just can't."

"Why?" asked Darren.

"Because," Harvey said, his voice rising, "I don't have any dry underpants!"

He sat down on a bed. "You go," he said. "I'll wait here."

"But … the photo shoot," said Darren.

Suddenly Professor Gertie's hand appeared in the doorway. Dangling from her fingers were the shiny red Fireproof  Underpants Harvey had worn with the Smoke Machine, one of Professor Gertie's first inventions for The Team.

"Harvey, please stop shouting and put these on," she said urgently. "Darren, you come with me. I can't be late again; I'm a 'Responsible Adult!'"

Harvey changed as fast as he could. But when he pulled on his shorts they were baggy and loose, and the ties were at the back, out of his reach. Holding them up with one hand, he raced to the field.

The teams were grouped on the small stage Harvey had seen from the bus. The Buffalos were squashed together on the left. The Termites were lined up neatly in the middle, and The Team were gathered on the right.

Harvey ran up just in time to hear the photographer introducing herself. He quickly squeezed into a space right at the front of The Team.

"I'm Karen Cascarino," the woman said, "but you can call me K.C. I've been sent from *Soccer Stars* magazine, and …"

Steffi screamed with delight. Harvey knew why. *Soccer Stars* was the top soccer magazine in the country.

"I'd like to begin with a group shot of all the teams," continued K.C. "Can the, er, Buffalos move back a bit so I can fit you in?"

The Buffalos shuffled back.

"The Termites can come closer, and," said K.C., pointing at Steffi, "can you please return to your team?"

Steffi was standing at the front of the stage with a dazzling smile on her face. "My name is Stefanie Bush," she said. "That's Stefanie with an 'f.'"

"Thank you, Miss Bush," said K.C., waiting patiently.

But Steffi didn't move, or stop smiling.

"What's up with Steffi?" Harvey whispered to Matt, but Matt just shook his head.

"Miss Bush!" said K.C. irritably as she crouched down to take the picture.

"Okay, okay," said Steffi sulkily. She

pushed her way back to her place, nearly jostling Harvey off the stage. "Move over!" she hissed.

"I can't," said Harvey. "There's no room."

Steffi tried to shove him out of the way with her elbow, and knocked his hand off his shorts, which fell all the way down to his ankles.

Click! Click! Click!

"Superb!" laughed K.C. Harvey saw her camera zoom in on his underpants.

"They're not mine!" he said desperately as everyone turned to see.

The Termites squealed.

"They're Professor Gertie's fireproof ones!" Harvey explained.

The Buffalos bellowed.

Harvey tried to make them understand. "I only wear them when I'm going to make smoke!"

The sound of the camera clicking was drowned out by bellowing and squealing.

Harvey wondered which would come out brightest in *Soccer Stars* magazine – his shiny underpants or his glowing face?

Chapter 4

"You're really funny," said K.C., holding Harvey's arm as he tried to get away after the photo shoot. "What's your name?"

"Harvey Bighead Boots!" yelled Steffi.

"It's not," said Harvey. "It's just Harvey Boots."

K.C. scribbled in her notebook. "Okay, Just Harvey Boots, have you always wanted to be a comedian?"

"No, he hasn't," hollered Steffi. "But he wants to steal the limelight from everyone else!"

"I wasn't trying to be funny," said Harvey. "I lost my bag so I didn't have any dry, er, things. Professor Gertie must have brought her Inventing Box with her. She gave me the, er, whatsits that I wear with the Smoke Machine."

"That's very interesting," said K.C.

"Who's Professor Gertie? What else has she invented?"

"I have to go!" said Harvey, and he bolted away, holding onto his shorts tightly. The last thing he wanted to do was talk about Professor Gertie's inventions, because then K.C. would find out about Mark 1.

Harvey found Darren, Matt and Rita waiting for him outside the huts.

"Hard luck, Harvey," said Darren.

"Rubbish," said Steffi, striding up to them. "Harvey's got K.C. begging for an interview. Talk about showing off!"

"What are you talking about?" asked Rita.

"This is a chance for all of us to be in *Soccer Stars*," said Steffi. "Not just Harvey."

"Why do you want to be in *Soccer Stars* so badly?" asked Darren.

Steffi rolled her eyes. "So I'd be famous, of course!"

"Famous for what?" Matt butted in. "You haven't done anything."

"Just famous!" said Steffi impatiently.

"Famous for being famous?" Matt laughed.

"Yes!" said Steffi. "Everybody wants to be famous."

The others looked at each other and shrugged.

"Harvey does," she said. "That's why he was joking around for K.C. This proves it." She picked up Harvey's bag, which was lying by the side of the hut as if someone had dropped it there.

"You probably hid it here yourself," Steffi said, throwing it to Harvey. "I bet you had those Fireproof Undies ready, too."

"I didn't!" Harvey protested. But Steffi turned her back on him and stalked off.

While Harvey checked his bag to make sure he had a spare pair of underpants, Darren admitted, "I wouldn't mind being famous for being a great goalie. Like, if I saved every shot for a year."

"That's being famous for doing something," said Rita. "Not just for being a pretty face."

Matt looked surprised. "Can you be famous for that? Cool!" He smiled the way Steffi did when K.C. was there.

"Sshh!" Professor Gertie tiptoed from the girls' hut. "Fame is a dangerous thing. If that woman finds out about Mark 1, she won't stop pestering us until she's got the whole story! We'll be exposed!"

"Why would she be interested in Mark 1?" asked Matt.

Professor Gertie glared at him. "Mark 1 is one of the most sophisticated robots ever made!" she said.

"And he's a soccer genius. He could fill a magazine all by himself!"

"Where is he now?" asked Harvey.

"Making himself invisible," said Professor Gertie.

Harvey heard heavy feet clomp down the steps of the boys' hut and turned around. Mark 1 looked the same as before, except for a yellow baseball cap that was stretched so tightly over his trashcan head it looked like a swimming cap.

The sound of Matt's laughter was drowned out by a long, piercing whistle.

"The game must be starting!" said Professor Gertie. "Harvey, go change your pants!"

Harvey ran inside to get changed. When he came out, he was relieved to see Professor Gertie waiting.

"I do hope Mark 1 keeps his head down," she said worriedly. "But I think he'll blend in now, don't you?"

As they arrived on the field, Harvey saw that Mark 1 definitely did not blend in. Even though he was standing with The Team all around him, the bright yellow cap made him stand out as if a spotlight were shining on his head. K.C. was already pushing past people to get to him.

"Hello!" Harvey heard her say. "You came with Harvey Boots, didn't you? What can you tell me about him? Does he have a girlfriend? And tell me about this Professor Gertie …"

Harvey listened anxiously, but the coach's voice drowned out Mark 1's replies.

"We play thirty minutes each half, with ten minutes in between," he said.

Harvey heard K.C. ask, "… and what else has she invented to help The Team? Apart from the Fireproof Underp –"

Professor Gertie nudged Harvey. "We have to stop her!" she said, her eyes bulging. The coach started speaking again before Harvey could respond.

"We'll be ready to start as soon as a line referee arrives," said the coach, looking around. "Is there anyone here with a yellow cap? All yellow-capped camp workers are fully trained referees. Aha! There's one!" The coach beckoned to Mark 1. "Don't just stand there!"

Harvey heard Professor Gertie groan as the coach put an orange flag into Mark 1's hand. "Oh no!" she said. "I found the cap in one of the huts! It's my fault!"

"The Team can kick off," said the coach as the players jogged onto the field.

Harvey joined Rita in the center and

watched K.C., who was standing on the sideline with Soccer Camp's newest line referee. While K.C. lifted what looked like a small telescope from her bag, Mark 1 pressed his chest. Harvey knew there was a button under Mark 1's shirt, and that pressing it once started his warm-up routine.

"I've got a very bad feeling about this," Harvey said as Mark 1 stretched and whirred, and K.C. began taking pictures. How many seconds would it be before they were found out? Harvey started counting to himself: one, two, three … He yelped as the coach blew

the whistle close to his ear.

"Kick off, Harvey!" called Matt from defense. "Let's see how many goals we can score before halftime!"

Harvey tapped the ball to Rita as energy flooded through him like it always did at the start of a game. His worries about Mark 1 floated to the back of his mind. Now was his chance to find out how good the Termites really were …

He didn't get another shot at the ball until ten long minutes later.

Chapter 5

They were like ants, Harvey decided. It didn't matter how small they were, because they were everywhere.

Whenever The Team got the ball, three or four Termites players swarmed in to retrieve it. Harvey was hoping they would soon run out of breath, but they showed no signs of tiring.

"This is embarrassing!" said Matt.

For the third time in a row, he'd lost the ball to a Termites forward right in front of Darren's goal. Darren came running out trying for yet another save, but there was nothing he could do as a Termites attacker chipped the ball neatly towards the open goal.

Harvey caught a glimpse of someone in a red shirt streaking across to intercept. At first, the sun shining yellow on the player's head gave Harvey the dreadful feeling that it was Mark 1 … but then he recognized Steffi's long blonde hair sailing out behind her.

With a flying kick, Steffi launched the ball upfield to Harvey, who immediately lost it to two Termites midfielders.

"Nice save!" Matt called to Steffi.

"Fantastic, more like!" said Darren.

Steffi didn't reply. Harvey saw that she was ignoring the game completely and smiling towards K.C., who was holding her camera ready.

Click!

The Termites launched a ferocious assault, and Harvey ran back to help The Team defend.

"I hope she gets me in some action shots," Steffi told him as he passed her. "Wait a minute; aren't you supposed to be attacking?"

"Yes!" said Harvey sharply. "But you're too busy posing to defend!"

It was useless. Harvey was too far behind the Termites forwards, who quickly hustled the ball through The Team defense. Again, Darren didn't stand a chance, and this time there was nobody to stop the ball from sailing into the goal.

"One-nothing to the Mites," huffed Matt. "Thanks to our most famous defender!" "We're lucky it isn't more," said Darren as The Team collapsed in the goal area at halftime. "They're running circles around us."

"They seem to read each other's minds," complained Rita.

"They work together," said Harvey simply. "They're a brilliant team."

For the rest of the break they watched Professor Gertie chasing after Mark 1, who was keeping one step ahead of her as he juggled his flag and cap. K.C. was snapping pictures of the two of them.

"Stop it!" they heard Professor Gertie shouting at Mark 1. "You're supposed to be incognito!"

"Poor Mark 1," said Rita. "He only wants to have some fun."

Harvey saw that the coach was ready to start. "Let's give it our best," he said to The Team encouragingly. "We haven't had a shot yet!"

Midway through the second half, with The Team still battling in defense, Rita managed to scoop the ball to Harvey's feet. He turned quickly and dodged two Termites midfielders.

There was no one to pass to, so he coasted down the right side of the field, giving The Team time to get forward. The Termites defense crowded him towards their corner flag, and to his frustration, Harvey found himself blocked in.

Suddenly he caught sight of a wave of red shirts breaking into the penalty area. The Team was on the attack! He fired the ball towards them, then watched glumly as it passed uselessly over their heads and curled towards the edge of the goal area. It looked to Harvey like it was going to land on Matt, who was the last to arrive.

"Look out, Matt!" he called.

Matt ducked, but he was too late. The ball slammed against the side of his head – and bounced straight into the top corner of the net!

"GOAL!" cried Professor Gertie.

Matt stumbled, rolled over twice and stood back up, looking dazed as Harvey raced across to congratulate him.

Click! Click! Click!

"Spectacular!" exclaimed K.C.

Matt grinned.

"Oh, you've got a perfect smile! But you're

not just a pretty
face, are you?"

Click! Click! Click!

Harvey saw that
Matt was still grinning
as he returned to The
Team defense.

The Termites kicked off, lost the ball to
Harvey, and retreated as The Team tried for
another goal.

"What's your name?" called K.C.

"Who, me?" asked Matt, who was hovering
by the halfway line. "I'm Matt."

"Matt what?"

He strolled over to the sideline. "Matt –"

"Stay in position!" hollered Harvey as he
was tackled.

The Termites counterattacked, bursting
through the gap Matt had left in defense. Matt
scrambled desperately for the ball, but the
Termites scurried past him and Darren for an
easy goal.

Matt groaned.

Click!

"That's more like you," snapped Steffi.
"*Soccer Stars* has a page at the back for
pictures like that, though usually they only
show people's ugly pets!"

From then on The Team had trouble
keeping the Termites from scoring again, and
Harvey was the lone striker as Rita bolstered
the defense. On the few occasions he got the
ball he had nobody to pass to, and the
Termites took it from him easily.

Harvey saw the coach put his whistle to
his mouth and call, "Last chance – everybody
forward!" He saw Mark 1 spring along the
sideline, his flag tucked under one arm,
making a noise like a rocket taking off.

Matt came tearing up the field, calling for
the ball and waving his arms like a windmill.
The rest of The Team were behind him,
streaming towards the Termites' goal. They
all knew that if they didn't score, they'd lose.

Defending was pointless now.

Steffi hassled the ball from a Termites defender, and sent it swerving into the goal area. Harvey quickened his pace ... but before he could reach the ball, another red-shirted player thundered in a diving header.

Harvey could hear the clicking of K.C.'s camera even over the shriek of the final whistle, and all his hope turned to dismay as The Team's "Responsible Adult" cartwheeled down the field to celebrate his stupendous goal.

Chapter 6

The coach held up a red card and spluttered, "Goal not allowed! Game over!" as Professor Gertie marched Mark 1 away. K.C. rushed after them, trailed by Steffi.

"Did you get a shot of my save off the line?" Harvey heard Steffi ask.

As Professor Gertie and Mark 1 disappeared behind the trees, K.C. stopped and turned towards Steffi.

"Looks like she's getting her interview," Rita observed. "Maybe she'll take K.C.'s mind off Mark 1," she added hopefully.

Harvey didn't reply. He was still standing in front of the goal, replaying the last move of the game in his mind. The ball coming across from Steffi, his clear opportunity ... he would probably have scored, he decided. If he had, The Team wouldn't have lost.

The coach was standing nearby, fuming and looking like he wanted to blow his whistle at somebody. "That was no line referee," Harvey heard him mutter.

"Let's go," Rita advised Harvey. As they followed the other teams back to the main building, she said, "I don't think we can fool the coach much longer. What are we going to do?"

Harvey felt depressed. "I just don't know," he said, sighing.

"This way," said Darren, holding a door open for them. "We get dinner inside. There's a cafeteria and everything."

They took trays from a kitchen hatch and looked for spaces to sit at one of the three long tables. Harvey spotted Professor Gertie at the furthest table, huddled behind the

leaves of a palm tree growing from a pot.

"Sorreee, Harvv," said Mark 1 from underneath the table when Harvey, Rita and Darren sat down. Harvey was pleased to find that Mark 1 was no longer wearing the yellow baseball cap.

But, he hated to see the robot looking so miserable behind his false glasses.

"That's okay," Harvey said. "And it was a good goal." He smiled, and Mark 1's eyes flickered happily.

Professor Gertie leaned across to Harvey. "I don't think anyone noticed he isn't actually a 'Responsible Adult.' But that woman with the camera is definitely getting suspicious. Look, there she is!"

Professor Gertie dove under the table as K.C. came in, closely followed by Steffi. "I don't know what to do!" Harvey heard Professor Gertie whining as she and Mark 1 crawled out through a side exit.

"Professor Gertie!" K.C. sailed towards their

table, and then stopped. "Oh, I thought I'd find Professor Gertie here," she said, turning to look meaningfully at Steffi, whose face had turned as red as the Fireproof Underpants. As K.C. walked away, Steffi kept at her heel.

"Did you see that?" Rita asked urgently. "You don't think Steffi would have told K.C. about Professor Gertie and Mark 1?"

"She'd better not have," said Harvey grimly, turning to his plate and playing with his food. He was worried about Mark 1, but he couldn't think of anything to do. Then the Buffalos sat down noisily at the next table, and Harvey started thinking about The Team's other big problem.

How were they ever going to beat the giant-sized Beefs?

Harvey lined up his meatballs. They were the Buffalos. Facing them, he made The Team out of peas and oddly shaped bits of carrot, with a mashed brussel sprout in goal. For the rest of dinner time, he pushed the players around on his plate. The meatballs were always too big. There was no way around them.

Darren nudged his shoulder. "We have to go," he said. They trailed behind the other teams into a large gymnasium, where they all sat on the floor in front of a television.

"A movie!" said Matt, who then groaned loudly when the words "Soccer Strategy" appeared on the screen.

The video showed bits from famous World Cup games. Harvey had seen some of them before. Every now and then the coach would stop the tape and say things like, "Play to your strengths. Winning teams do what they're good at."

The room was hot, and everyone began to doze, even Harvey. Watching wasn't giving him any ideas, and he was relieved when the teams were at last led back to their huts.

Harvey lay down on his bed and closed his eyes. As the others began to snore, he tried to relax. "If K.C. finds out about Mark 1," he thought to himself, "at least we won't have to play the Buffalos. We'll be going home instead!"

Harvey was soon dreaming that the *Soccer Stars* reporter was following him everywhere, longing to know the secret of Mark 1. She was spoiling everything he did by bugging him with questions. Harvey tugged his blankets over his head, and kept undercover …

Chapter 7

Harvey felt his covers being yanked away and tried to hold on. "No pictures!" he screeched, before realizing it wasn't K.C.

"It's me," said Darren as everyone around them laughed. "The coach just told us that breakfast is ready, and there'll be nothing left if we don't get a move on."

Harvey pulled on his uniform, trying to shake off his dream, but he couldn't help checking all the windows to make sure K.C. wasn't spying on him. Then, as he left the hut, he spotted her running along the path to the main building. She was heading towards Professor Gertie and Mark 1, who appeared to have no idea they were being followed.

Harvey pelted after them, ignoring calls from Darren. Professor Gertie and Mark 1 rounded the corner of the building, and K.C. dashed around after them.

Harvey reached the turn seconds later, skidded around, and found … nobody.

He ran to the big glass doors and pushed them open. There was just an empty office. He checked the cafeteria, then the gym. There was no sign of Professor Gertie, Mark 1 or K.C.

Darren arrived, with Rita close behind.

"What's the matter?" panted Rita. "Why did you take off like that?"

"K.C. followed Professor Gertie and Mark 1 here," said Harvey. "Now they've all disappeared."

"They must be hiding," said Darren. "They could be anywhere."

"What's going on?" demanded Steffi,

marching up to them. "Are you talking about me?"

"No," said Rita. "Should we be?"

Steffi opened her mouth to say something, but no words came out.

"How come you're so cozy with K.C. all of a sudden?" Rita pressed her. "You didn't tell her about Mark 1, did you?"

Steffi's face turned pink.

"You did!" said Rita, aghast.

"I told her my life story," Steffi said defiantly. "And Mark 1 is part of it, that's all. *Soccer Stars* readers deserve the truth."

She turned on her heel and walked away, leaving her three teammates staring after her with shocked expressions.

Harvey felt numb. "That's it," he said. "We're done for."

"I saw K.C. with the coach during the video last night," said Darren. "They were whispering about something."

Harvey sighed as the smell of cooking wafted from the cafeteria.

"We might as well eat something before the long bus ride home," he said gloomily.

While they ate, the rest of The Team joined them, talking enthusiastically about the games ahead. Harvey felt miserable. How could he tell his friends that their time at Soccer Camp was about to end?

Suddenly the coach came in and blew a short "pip!" on his whistle. Everyone fell silent. Harvey felt his stomach sinking. The coach held up a ball and said, "The Termites play the Buffalos in thirty minutes.

After that we'll have a drink break, then the
Buffalos play The Team."

Darren gave Harvey the thumbs up, grinning.

Harvey felt relief flood through him.
"Why hasn't K.C. told the coach about
Mark 1?" he asked Rita.

"Maybe she's keeping it to herself," said
Rita, "for a *Soccer Stars* exclusive story."

Harvey imagined a picture of himself and
Mark 1 in the magazine and, to his surprise,
he felt his spirits rise. It wouldn't be so bad if
he wasn't in there alone. He took a hungry
bite of toast.

"Now that leaves us with one tiny little
problem," said Rita.

"What's that?" asked Harvey.

"If we want to win the Soccer Camp Cup," said Rita, "we have to beat the Buffalos. But don't worry – I have a feeling they're just big, slow and clumsy."

After breakfast, everyone headed to the field, and The Team sat down to watch as the Buffalos plowed easily through the Termites.

"It's a massacre," said Rita after the Beefs had powered in their first goal. The Termites goalie had been knocked flat on his back, and there was an oversized cleat print on his chest.

Darren looked pale. "What are we going to do?" he asked Harvey.

Matt leaned across and said cheerily,

"We're going to win, of course."

"And how are we supposed to do that?" asked Rita.

"Harvey's got a plan," said Matt.

"Huh?" said Harvey. "What plan? I don't have a plan!"

"You watched that video last night," said Matt. "You must have some ideas."

The Team all turned eagerly to Harvey.

"I think," he said weakly, "that we have to play to our strengths."

"And what are they?" asked Steffi, coming over from where she'd been sitting on her own.

Harvey looked at his friends. What *were* their strengths? They weren't small and quick like the Termites, or big and strong like the Buffalos. Matt and Steffi were both good defenders, but they didn't play the same way. Steffi was fast and aggressive. Matt was slow and patient, only tackling when the time was right.

"We're all different," Harvey said at last, shrugging.

"Great," said Steffi disgustedly. "We don't have any strengths. Remind me to tell K.C. when she gets here. We don't want her to make a mistake when she writes about us in *Soccer Stars*."

Rita looked angrily at Steffi, but before she could say anything there was a loud roar as the Buffalos blasted home their second goal. The Team watched the rest of the game in moody silence.

Every now and then Harvey stood up and looked around, but he didn't see Professor Gertie, Mark 1 or K.C. anywhere.

"The Termites didn't do too badly," said Rita when the coach blew the final whistle, and the Buffalos gave a victory bellow. "They only lost three-nothing. We should be able to tie, at least."

"You're forgetting that we lost to the Termites," said Harvey. "The Buffalos are going to slaughter us."

"And," added Darren, "The Team are in last place because we're the only ones who haven't won yet."

Rita looked crestfallen as they grabbed drinks from trays brought around by the Soccer Camp workers.

"Remember, everyone," urged Matt, who had unexpectedly stood up to address The Team, "we need to win by three goals. If you want my advice, keep the pressure on until we're winning at least four-nothing."

"I think scoring a goal has gone to his head," said Darren after Matt sat down, "but at least one of us is happy."

"I think we should just try to be ourselves, and do our own thing," said Rita. "What's the worst that could happen?"

"We'll lose," said Darren and Harvey together.

"Oh, big deal!" Rita said loudly. And when Harvey choked on his drink, spilling it on his shirt, both she and Darren laughed.

"Professor Gertie won't be happy cleaning that!" said Darren.

"It doesn't matter," Harvey said with a grin. "Supercloth cleans itself, doesn't it?"

He wiped the liquid from his shirt with his hand. It came off bubbly and pink. "This drink's weird," he said.

Just then, the coach called the teams over to start the last game of Soccer Camp, and Harvey sprang lightly to his feet. The time for worrying was over.

Chapter 8

The first five minutes of the game against the Buffalos were the hardest The Team had ever known. The Beefs began their attack slowly, but soon sped up into a stampede. It was dangerous to get in their way.

"Oof!" breathed Harvey as he was knocked sideways and landed on his face.

He lay stunned for a few seconds before painfully pushing himself to his feet, and looking downfield at The Team milling around in defense.

They were just like the peas and carrots he had pushed around his plate the evening before. They didn't stand a chance. The meatballs were unstoppable.

A Buffalos striker shot, and Darren pushed the ball away for a corner kick. As The Team took their usual positions to defend, Harvey imagined mashing up his peas and carrots with a fork, changing them into something new and unrecognizable – something unexpected.

"Swap!" he shouted suddenly. "Matt, Steffi – everyone in defense change positions!"

The Team stared at him, puzzled.

"Are you sure?" asked Rita.

"Won't that be, er, confusing?" asked Darren.

"Do it!" said Matt, who was shoving Steffi out of his way to take her spot on the goal line. "This is Harvey's PLAN!"

The Team's defense reluctantly swapped places with each other. Harvey thought that the Buffalos were looking more confused than The Team.

When the ball came in from the corner, Matt cleared it by darting courageously between two huge forwards.

"They weren't expecting my pretty face!" Matt declared proudly. "Great strategy, Harv!"

From then on, The Team defense changed positions for every Buffalos attack.

"I don't believe it," Rita told Harvey, shaking her head. "But I think you've found a way to stop them!"

The Team began to put pressure on the Buffalos' goal. Harvey made a run, and Rita tried a long cross, but it was useless. The Beefs tall goalkeeper reached over Harvey's head and caught the ball.

"Crosses are no good," Harvey told The Team at halftime.

"Any idea how to score?" asked Rita.

"None," admitted Harvey.

"Me neither," said Rita.

As The Team kicked off the second half, Harvey was relieved to see Professor Gertie

and Mark 1 arrive. And to his surprise, K.C. was with them. In fact, the three of them seemed quite friendly.

What was going on?

"Go for it, Mr. Boots!" K.C. called, pointing her camera at him.

Harvey, who was looking towards K.C., had the ball taken from him. He turned back to the game as the Buffalos charge was again halted by The Team changing defense.

"If we could only score," Harvey said to Rita as she sprinted past to receive the ball, "I think we could win!"

Rita threaded the ball to Harvey, and he ran at the Buffalos defense.

Almost like he was inside a pinball machine, he rebounded from one giant defender to the next.

Rita tried a run herself, but she was squashed by two Buffalos players halfway towards their goal. The coach awarded a free kick, and she placed the ball carefully on the grass.

"Don't bother crossing!" Harvey reminded her, but it looked like that was exactly what Rita was planning.

Harvey tried to find space among the Buffalos defenders, but there was barely room to move. The keeper came right out of his goal and stood behind Harvey with his hands held up, ready to catch the ball.

"They know what you're going to do!" Harvey shouted, but it was too late. Rita was already stepping up to the ball, and she booted it long and high. It whizzed wide to the right of Harvey. He heard the Buffalos goalie gasp, saw Rita raise her arms, and then spun around in time to watch the ball

bounce into the Buffalos' unguarded goal.

"Yes!" Harvey whispered, his voice rising to a delighted cry. "Yes!"

"They weren't expecting a shot on goal!" said Darren as The Team lifted Rita off her feet.

"Nobody was!" said Harvey.

"Except me!" Rita corrected them. "I knew what I was going to do all along. Now put me down!"

For the rest of the match, the Buffalos were forced to defend their goal, and despite The Team's efforts the score stayed the same. The Team won one-nothing.

"Well done," said the coach briskly as The Team congratulated each other. "You worked together, and everyone was allowed to play to their own strengths."

"And," he added, goggling at Mark 1 as the robot twirled Rita above his head, "The Team are full of surprises."

K.C. appeared at Harvey's side with her notebook in her hand. "Harvey Boots," she said. "You haven't won the Camp Cup, but you have beaten the Buffalos. How do you feel at this moment?"

"Er, great!" said Harvey, and then, unable to help himself, he posed for the camera.

Click!

Chapter 9

K.C. arranged the teams in the center circle, the coach hung medals around all the players' necks, and the Buffalos were presented with the Soccer Camp Cup.

"Each team won a game," Matt explained to Harvey, "but the Beefs scored the most goals."

Click!

K.C. wrote down each of the Buffalos' names.

Then, she closed her notebook, held up her camera and asked Harvey, "Got any more jokes, Mr. Boots? I only have one shot left."

Harvey shook his head.

The *Soccer Stars* reporter pretended to sulk, then stood back to frame everyone. "Smile, champs!"

Harvey felt a familiar drumming of water on his skull as the sprinklers rained down on them, but he didn't move. Nobody did. They were all holding their smiles as they waited for K.C. to take their picture.

The camera suddenly jerked towards The Team, and Harvey automatically put his hands to his shorts. Luckily, though, this time they hadn't fallen down, and he looked around to see who else had done something embarrassing.

Harvey started to giggle.

The Team were giving off bubbles! White bubbles from their shorts, and pink bubbles from their shirts.

Professor Gertie had her mouth open wide. "Oh!" she said. "It's my Supercloth! It never needs washing so I never tested it with water!"

The Team were nearly hidden in a mountain of soapsuds, and when K.C. finally took her last shot of Soccer Camp – *click* – Harvey Boots was laughing loudest of all.

One week later The Team were in Professor Gertie's inventing tower, their eyes fixed on a large envelope. Darren read the message scrawled along the bottom.

"Thanks for being fun Soccer Stars! Love, K.C."

Professor Gertie tore it open and held up the magazine. On the front there was a picture of the coach blowing his whistle.

"So that's why he was whispering with K.C. during the video!" said Rita. "Is everyone obsessed by fame?"

"Come on, look inside!" Steffi reached forward, turned the page, and gasped when a large picture of Professor Gertie smiled out at them.

Rita read, "Inventor and Soccer Fan, Professor Gertie Gallop tells Karen Cascarino about her inventing box of tricks."

Steffi snatched the magazine and began skimming through it. It was full of Professor Gertie and her inventions. At least half the pages were about Mark 1.

"YEP SSSIR!" the robot whooped, punching the air.

Steffi turned furiously to Professor Gertie. "K.C. was supposed to put me in *Soccer Stars*, but it's all about you! I thought you said fame was dangerous!"

"I met K.C. on the way to breakfast that last morning," explained Professor Gertie, blushing as she took the magazine back and began to read it. "She said you had already told her about Mark 1 and me, and I just wanted to give her the full story. I suppose everyone wants a little bit of celebrity," she added with a guilty grin.

"I don't," said Harvey, who was nervously scanning the pages as Professor Gertie turned them. Any time now, he thought, I'll see my underpants.

He didn't have long to wait.

There they were, in the center of the magazine, in full color. There was even a dotted line around them, so they could be cut out.

Darren read, "Are these The Team's latest secret weapon?"

Harvey glanced up to where he expected to see his own embarrassed face, and almost collapsed with laughter.

"Look who's famous!" cackled Matt.

"Well done!" said Darren. "You've really made it, Steffi!"

Where Harvey's face should have been, there was a shot of Steffi flashing her biggest, brightest smile.

STEFFI

"It does serve you right, Steffi," Rita said coolly. "That's what happens to people who'd do anything for fame."

Harvey thought Steffi would see the funny side eventually. That is, when she finally stopped screaming.

Professor
Gertie

Darren

Harvey

Rita

Matt

Steffi

Mark 1

About the Authors

David Bedford was born in Devon, in the southwest of England, in 1969.

David wasn't always a writer – first he was a soccer player! He played for two teams: Appleton Football Club and Sankey Rangers. Although these weren't the worst teams in the league, they never won anything! David was also a scientist. His first job was in the United States, where he worked on discovering new antibiotics.

But, David always loved to read and he decided to start writing stories himself. After a few years, he left his job as a scientist and began writing full time. He now has 10 books published, which have been translated into many languages around the world.

David lives with his wife and daughter in Norfolk, England.

Keith Brumpton has written and illustrated over 35 humorous books for children. He also writes scripts and screenplays. Keith now lives in Glasgow, Scotland.